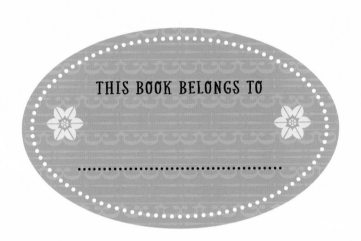

THIS BOOK BELONGS TO

....

SNOW WHITE

Written by Helen Anderton

Illustrated by Stuart Lynch

make believe ideas

Reading together

This book is designed to be fun for children who are learning to read. The simple sentences avoid abbreviations and are written in the present tense. The big type also helps children with their word-shape recognition.

Take some time to discuss the story with your child. Here are some ways you can help your child take those first steps in reading:

❋ Encourage your child to look at the pictures and talk about what is happening in the story.

❋ Help your child to find familiar words.

❋ Ask your child to read and repeat each short sentence.

❋ Try using some of the following questions as you go along:
  • What do you think will happen next?
  • Do you like this character?
  • What kind of voice would this character have?

Sound out the words

Encourage your child to sound out the letters in any words he or she doesn't know. Look at the key words listed at the back of the book and see which of them your child can find on each page.

Reading activities

The **What happens next?** activity encourages your child to retell the story and point to the mixed-up pictures in the right order.

The **Rhyming words** activity takes six words from the story and asks your child to read and find other words that rhyme with them.

The **Key words** pages provide practice with common words used in the context of the book. Read the sentences with your child and encourage him or her to make up more sentences using the key words listed around the border.

A **Picture dictionary** page asks children to focus closely on nine words from the story. Encourage your child to look carefully at each word, cover it with his or her hand, write it on a separate piece of paper, and finally, check it!

Do not complete all the activities at once – doing one each time you read will ensure that your child continues to enjoy the story and the time you are spending together. Have fun!

Snow White lives with a pretty queen. The queen asks her mirror who is fairest of all.

The mirror says the queen is the fairest. This makes the queen happy.

One day the mirror says
that Snow is the fairest.

The queen gets angry.

The queen sends Snow away.

Snow runs into the woods.

The woods are dark
and scary. Some dwarfs
get off a bus. They ask
Snow to live with them.

13

Snow is happy with the dwarfs. She cooks them food and cleans the house.

In the castle, the queen is angry. She puts an apple in some poison.

The queen dresses in a hood.
She gives Snow the apple.

Snow bites the apple
and falls down.

The dwarfs put
Snow in a glass case.
Then a prince sees her . . .

The prince kisses Snow.
Snow wakes up!

The mirror still says that Snow is the fairest.

The queen throws
the mirror away.

Snow and the prince live
happily ever after.

What happens next?

Some of the pictures from the story have been mixed up! Can you retell the story and point to each picture in the correct order?

Rhyming words

Read the words in the middle of each group and point to the other words that rhyme with them.

bean   **queen**   mean

trees   woods

apple   **snow**   flow

grow   house

book   **cook**   mice

hook   prince

dwarf

girl

down

frown

town

clean

kiss

prince

since

wince

cloak

face

case

hood

place

Now choose a word and make up a rhyming chant!

The **mean queen** smells like **beans!**

Key words

These sentences use common words to describe the story. Read the sentences and then make up new sentences for the other words in the border.

The queen **asks** the mirror questions.

The mirror **says** Snow White is fairest.

Snow runs **into** the woods.

Some dwarfs get **off** a bus.

Snow cleans the dwarfs' **house**.

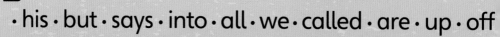

like · asks

· his · but · says · into · all · we · called · are · up · off

queen makes
poisoned apple.

The queen
gives Snow
the apple.

The dwarfs
keep Snow
in a case.

The prince kisses
Snow and she
wakes **up**.

Snow and the
prince **live** happily
ever after.

the · and · to · not · live · a · him · I · of · it · went · got · in · on · big · is · for

house · meets · back · put · this · about · so · be ·

Picture dictionary

Look carefully at the pictures and the words.
Now cover the words, one at a time.
Can you remember how to write them?

apple

bus

castle

dwarf

hood

kiss

mirror

poison

woods